Listen to the music for Foggy
(and download it, too!)
at www.simplyreadbooks.com.

First published in 2009 by Simply Read Books
www.simplyreadbooks.com

Characters, set design, art direction, and dioramas
by Robin Mitchell-Cranfield & Judith Steedman
Colour separations by Scanlab

Library and Archives Canada Cataloguing in Publication
Mitchell, Robin, 1975-
     Foggy / Robin Mitchell-Cranfield & Judith Steedman.
ISBN 978-1-894965-96-5
     I. Steedman, Judith II. Title.
PS8576.I8865F64 2009   jC813'.6
C2009-900912-9

We gratefully acknowledge for their financial support
of our publishing program the Canada Council for
the Arts, the BC Arts Council, and the Government of
Canada through the Book Publishing Industry
Development Program (BPIDP).

WE WOULD ESPECIALLY LIKE TO THANK

Kallie George & Gillian Hunt for their editing assistance

Brady Cranfield for producing the "Foggy" compilation

Everyone who performed on the "Foggy" compilation

THIS BOOK IS DEDICATED WITH MUCH LOVE TO

Henry & Tova

FIND OUT MORE ABOUT WINDY AT

www.windyandfriends.com

SIMPLY READ BOOKS

Cloud and his dog

Foggy

Illustrations by
Robin Mitchell-Cranfield & Judith Steedman

This book belongs to ―――――――――

Nautical Knots

 overhand knot

 figure eight knot

 square knot

Red sky at night,
Sailors' delight.

Red sky at morning,
Sailors take warning.

On a dewy spring morning, Cloud and his dog, Foggy, looked out from their cozy tent to watch the red dawn fade to blue.

"Foggy, what did my Sailor's Handbook say? I think it said:

Red sky at morning,
Sailors go exploring.

"That's it! A perfect day for a sail."

Cloud buttoned his coat and put on his boots. Foggy brushed his ears and readied the sail.

They launched their boat and off they set.

Their feet and paws were barely wet when a fog rolled in.

"Can you see anything in this fog?" asked Cloud.

A small green spot with two big eyes appeared in view.

What could it be?

"Ah, it's a frog!"

"We're lost. Can you help us?"

"Certainly not," said the frog. "I'm very busy." And off he hopped.

The fog grew thicker
and thicker.

"What are those lights?"

"Traffic lights and street lamps. We've reached the city!"

They waved to Sunny and Gale as they sailed by.

"So long!"

But no sooner had they left the city than the fog rolled in again.

"Oh, Foggy. We're really in a pickle now."

Through the fog they heard a gentle hoot and a splash. Who was there?

It was Windy and Old Al.

Windy was making a map of the cove.

"Ahoy, Windy. We keep getting lost in this fog!"

"Here is a map to help you find your way home," offered Windy.

They thanked Windy and Old Al and set sail again.

Surveying the map, it was
easy to see where they were.

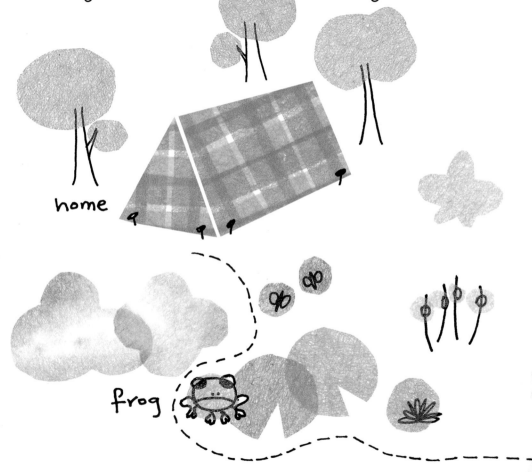

old al

windy

the city

"Quick!
  The compass,
  the telescope,
  we're almost home."

"Land ho!"

Back at camp, Cloud checked his Sailor's Handbook. It said:

**Red sky at morning,
Sailors take warning.**

"So it wasn't the perfect day for a sail after all! But it was the perfect day for a foggy adventure."

Cloud and Foggy roasted marshmallows until their socks were dry and it was time for bed.

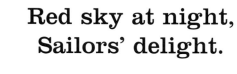

Red sky at night,
Sailors' delight.

Goodnight, Cloud.
Goodnight, Foggy.